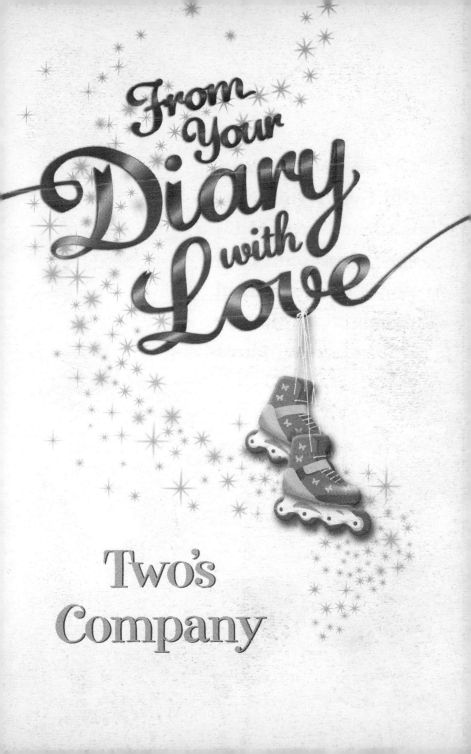

From Your Diary with Love

Two's Company

On her tenth birthday,
shy Evie Denham's life
is turned around by a
special present. In the
pages of a beautiful
purple diary lies the
key to her happiness . . .

When her family moves from London to the little town of Crossacre, talented dancer Evie finds it difficult to settle in to her new life. On Evie's birthday, her mysterious neighbour, Mrs Volkov, gives her a beautiful purple velvet diary as a present But this is no ordinary journal: every time Evie pens an entry and tucks it under her pillow overnight, she discovers the book has written back the following morning with words of guidance. Evie's diary soon becomes her treasured friend, holding the secret to her finding her feet in Crossacre, and giving her the confidence to do what she does best:

dance!

This diary is for you alone,
A secret you must keep,
Each night, tell me your worries,
And then fall sound asleep.

And as the dawn sun wakes you up,
The answer will be here,
Some words to help and guide you,
So you need have no fear.

Evie, please keep me safe and hidden,
For if anyone finds out,
These words will fade, and I'll be gone.
Of this there is no doubt.

And later, when my work is done,
Please don't put me aside.
Pass me on, wish me goodbye,
And someone else I'll guide.

Special thanks to:
Joanna Tubbs, West Jesmond Primary School, Maney Hill
Primary School and Courthouse Junior School

EGMONT
We bring stories to life

Two's Company first published in Great Britain 2008
by Egmont UK Limited
239 Kensington High Street, London W8 6SA

Text & illustration © 2008 Egmont UK Ltd
Text by Joanna Tubbs
Illustrations by Mélanie Florain

ISBN 978 1 4052 3952 3

1 3 5 7 9 10 8 6 4 2

A CIP catalogue record for this title is available
from the British Library

Typeset by Avon DataSet Ltd, Bidford on Avon, Warwickshire
Printed and bound in Great Britain by the CPI Group

From Your Diary with Love

Two's Company

EGMONT

The Denham Family

Charlie Denham

He's Evie's cool older brother who has lots of friends at school and loves playing sport, but always finds time to look out for his little sister

Evie Denham

Evie is a shy, quiet girl but with a little help and advice she hopes to make all her dancing dreams come true

Evie's Mum

She's a nurse at the local hospital and is keen for her children to feel at home in Crossacre

Evie's Dad

He's happy to have escaped city life, and when he's not enjoying the quiet surroundings of Crossacre he's running his own Internet business

Josh Denham

He's Evie's little brother. He can be a nosy pest a lot of the time, but he loves Evie really and looks up to her a lot

The Malkova Dance Academy
Students and Staff

Lottie Dean
Thinks she's the star of The Malkova Dance Academy

Meera Stevens
Evie's friend and a talented artist

Mrs Violet Swann
She's the wise principal of the dance academy who her pupils look up to

Jess Whittington
Evie's friend and a hard worker

Dame Malkova

The legendary prima ballerina
who founded the academy
and who still manages to inspire
the students years later

Lauren Davies

Evie's friend and
a natural athlete

Miss Connie Swann

She's a beautiful and kind
dance teacher who always
inspires her students

Matt Shanklin

He's the only
boy at the
academy and a
reluctant dancer

Beth Dickinson

She's Evie's best
friend and excellent
at modern dance

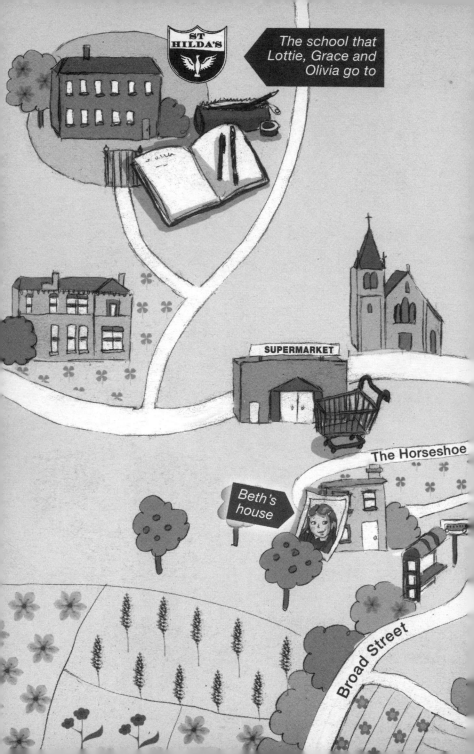

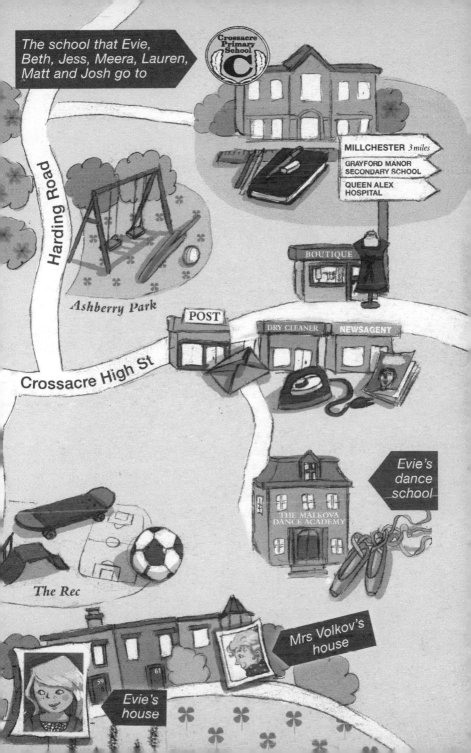

Contents

Chapter One

Three's a Crowd

Evie had spent the whole afternoon in the sitting room trying to read her new *Ballet Magic* magazine. Unfortunately, her little brother Josh and his best friend, Owen, were playing their *Frantic Football* card game.

'Goal!' yelled Josh gleefully, throwing down his last card.

'Disallowed!' screamed Owen, slapping a

referee card on top.

'That's not fair! I was out!'

'But you started first, so I've got one more go!'

Mum came in just as Evie, with a cushion pressed over each ear, wailed 'Pleeease shut up!'

'Come on, Evie, love,' Mum said, and led her to the quiet of the kitchen. 'How do you fancy inviting Beth round? She can join us for tea then you could watch a film or something.'

'Thanks, Mum,' said Evie. 'That would be brilliant! I *so* need a break from those two!'

Beth arrived as Dad was phoning out for a gigantic teatime pizza, and soon Evie's miserable afternoon turned into a real treat.

They were sitting on the stairs trying to decide what to do, when the pizza-delivery bike stopped outside. Beth grinned and gave Evie a nudge.

'Let's play a trick!' she said, and ran to the front door. Just as the boy was about to knock they yanked it open and screamed. The poor boy was so shocked he almost dropped the pizza, and they ran away giggling while Dad apologised and paid the bill.

'Mmm, this is good!' said Mum as they sat round the table.

'Well, I'm a very talented cook,' said Dad.

'Ha, ha,' said Evie, then whispered to Beth, 'Sorry, he always says that!'

'Oh, I nearly forgot,' said Dad. 'I'm bagging the TV this evening. There's an interesting programme about pensions I'd like to see. You can watch it too, if you like.'

'That's *really* kind of you,' said Evie, 'but I think we'll go to my room.'

For a while, they sat on Evie's bed playing CDs and chatting about their morning ballet lesson at The Malkova Dance Academy.

Then Beth's favourite song came on. She jumped up, grabbed Evie's hairbrush for a microphone, and began to sing along. Evie joined in immediately, cupping her hands over her ears like studio headphones and swaying to the tune.

'Hey!' said Beth when the CD finished. 'Why don't we make up our own dance?'

'Yes!' said Evie excitedly. 'We'll need more room, though.'

'Could we push your bed against the wall?'

'Good idea!' said Evie. 'You take that end.'

They shoved it across the floor, but Evie's hand caught her pillow, revealing the purple cover of an old book. Quickly, she covered it up, hoping

Beth hadn't spotted it – she couldn't let anyone, not even her closest friend in Crossacre, discover the secret of that book. It was her special diary.

With the floor clear, Evie pressed 'play' and Beth began to dance. As she tried all sorts of slides and turns, Evie scribbled everything down on a notepad. Then they swapped round, with Beth calling out the steps as Evie matched the routine exactly to the music.

At the end of the song Evie felt puffed out, so they swapped again.

'For this routine,' said Evie in a posh announcer's voice, 'you must dance in the style of Miss Lottie Dean.'

Beth leaped up, smiling like a beauty queen, and bowed. Then she flounced, strutted and waved her arms around with such exaggerated

flourishes that Evie fell off the bed laughing!

Suddenly, there came a knock and the door flew open. There stood Josh wearing Dad's hat and coat, and Owen with a felt-tip pen moustache, carrying Mum's umbrella. They marched into the room and sat on Evie's bed.

'We are the judges!' said Josh.

'And we think your dance is pants!' Owen added.

'So you are sentenced to a million years in prison!' said Josh.

'GET OUT!' shouted Evie, shoving them on to the landing and slamming the door behind them, then propping a chair against the door. 'Shall we start again from the top?'

They turned the volume up full and began slowly. Then something clicked: each step

7

synchronised perfectly, their timing was spot-on, every move rolled seamlessly to the next.

'Yayyyy! That was brilliant!' gasped Beth.

'Let's –' said Evie, but stopped dead with her mouth open. Dad's head was poking round the door and he *must* have seen them dancing!

'I knocked,' he shouted, holding out the phone, 'but you didn't hear. Anyway, it's Hannah for you.'

Instantly forgetting her embarrassment, Evie grabbed the handset.

'Hannah! How are you?'

Beth paused the CD and sat on the bed, kicking her legs.

'I know! I can't believe it!' Evie squealed into the phone. 'All day together in London! It'll be fantastic!'

After ten minutes of wondering if the call could possibly last any longer, Beth stood up. Obviously,

it could! She pressed 'stop' on the CD player and stared out the window.

'And when we've finished the shops,' Evie continued, 'Mum said we might go to a show! Which one do you fancy?'

Beth crossed her arms and frowned . . . but Evie, smiling happily, was so excited she didn't notice.

Chapter Two

The Perfect Plan

Evie hurried to school, her diary's latest message playing on her mind. She pictured the curled writing in her head, its words tinged with a gentle warning:

Although you're excited about your big plans for the weekend, remember that not everyone feels the same way. Indeed, it could be making someone close to you feel left out.

Evie realised that her constant chatter about her weekend with Hannah might be having an effect on Beth. She hated to think that her friend was feeling unhappy. Hannah would always be special, but Evie's new friends were important, too.

It wasn't long ago that Evie was the newest girl at Crossacre Primary School, with no one to talk to, so she knew exactly what it was like to feel left out in the cold. She simply had to make sure that Beth was all right.

If only Hannah and Beth knew each other they would understand that they're both special to me, she thought.

Over the past couple of days, Evie had been working on an idea that she hoped would make Beth smile again. She had spoken to her mum endlessly about it to make sure that all the details were in place. She had even phoned Hannah to check it out with her, too. Now all she had to do was to let Beth herself know.

She's going to love it! Evie thought, walking as fast as she could to reach the playground before the bell rang for registration.

Evie ran through the school gates and searched the playground for Beth's familiar red coat. *There she is*, she thought, spotting a little huddle of girls sitting on a bench in a sheltered corner. Her heart beat faster as she dashed over to her friends, unable to hold back her exciting plan for a second longer.

'Hi, everyone!' she said with a huge grin. 'Beth, I don't want you to feel left out so why don't you

just come to London with me and Hannah tomorrow, OK?' Evie's words spilled out in a jumble and Beth sat on the bench, opening and closing her mouth like a surprised goldfish. *Oh, dear*, thought Evie, her cheeks reddening. *That didn't come out right. I didn't mean it to sound as if Beth should be grateful!*

'Wow, Beth, that sounds fantastic!' said Jess. But Beth was lost for words.

'Um, I'm not sure,' she said at last. 'I think I'm busy.'

'*What?*' said Meera, stunned at her friend's response. 'You usually *love* going on adventures like that, Beth.'

'A day out shopping on Oxford Street sounds *totally* glamorous!' added Lauren. 'What are you doing that is more important than that?'

'I, um, I think maybe my grandma's coming over,' said Beth, who didn't sound too sure.

'OK, don't worry about it then,' said Evie, keen to change the subject. She felt embarrassed and upset by Beth's reaction and she just wanted to avoid talking about it any longer. 'Is it her birthday? Are you going to go out for lunch?'

'I don't know, all right?' snapped Beth. It didn't sound like she wanted to discuss the weekend at all.

'Your plans sound brilliant, Evie!' said Meera. 'Tell us all about the trendy shops you're going to.'

Jess nodded eagerly. 'Oh, yes, I'd love to hear about it! A day out in London – you're so lucky!' she added.

Evie knew she shouldn't talk about it too much in front of Beth when she obviously felt funny about it all. But she couldn't help being excited and, before long, she was spilling out all of her plans for the big day on Saturday. As she told

Lauren, Jess and Meera about the brilliant burger restaurant her mum had booked for lunch and all the birthday money she had saved to spend on Oxford Street, her excitement began to surge up again. As she gushed about Hannah's ideas for what to buy and where to visit, Beth sat quietly on the bench.

When the bell rang, Beth leaped up and practically sprinted to the classroom door.

'Wait for us!' cried Meera. Beth was usually last to be ready, spending ages scrabbling about in her bag and fiddling with her shoelaces. But today, it seemed she couldn't wait to get away from Evie's weekend plans and stories about the wonderful Hannah.

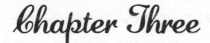

Chapter Three

Girls' Day Out

'You'll be glad you wore those trainers after a couple of hours walking around the shops,' Evie's mum said as they found their seats on the train. They had got up extra early to catch the half past eight train from Millchester to London and had a busy day of shopping and gossiping ahead of them.

Evie had tried to persuade her mum that her

19

sparkly ballet pumps were just as comfortable, but in the end she knew that trainers were the right choice. Mrs Denham had packed her roomiest handbag with extra jumpers and a bottle of water each, and they were all set to hit the city.

'Isn't it exciting, love?' said Mrs Denham. 'A girls' day out. It's a shame Beth couldn't make it, but maybe another time, eh?'

Evie thought of Beth with a pang of guilt. She and the other girls would be getting ready for ballet just about now, squeezing into their practice leotards and slipping on their satin shoes ready for warm-up. *I hope I don't miss anything important*, she thought, picturing Miss Connie leading her friends through a dainty routine.

Evie had been going to dance classes every Saturday for years, and it felt strange to be missing out. But she still managed to feel excited about the day ahead, despite a little wave of anxiety that ran through her when she thought of the dancing and giggling that was going on back in Crossacre.

When her mum pulled out a magazine, Evie knew that she'd be lost in the world of celebrity gossip for a good while. It was the perfect opportunity for her to have a little peek at her diary. Evie had been waiting to hear what it had

to say about the awkward conversation she'd had with Beth the day before. She reached into her bag and felt a silvery tingle run up her arm as she touched its rich covering.

She pulled it on to her lap and opened it a crack. Beautiful handwriting covered the page once again.

Dear Evie,

You mustn't worry about what happened yesterday. It might not have seemed like it at the time but maybe, deep down, I'm sure Beth was pleased that you offered to share your special weekend with her. Perhaps she was surprised by the sudden offer and a bit nervous about getting involved in such an old, strong friendship.

Try to remember that every person can

*offer something different to you. Every
friendship is unique and cannot be replaced.*

Suddenly, Mrs Denham burst out laughing,
making Evie jump. She slammed her diary shut
before she reached the end of the note.

'Ooh, will you listen to this, Evie!' she said.
'*Which celebrity was spotted leaving his mother's house
carrying a teddy and wearing a "Mummy's little soldier"
T-shirt?*' she read from her magazine.

'I don't know,' said Evie, giggling more about
her mum's sudden interest in celebrities than the
silly story itself.

Soothed by her diary's advice, Evie put her
worries about Beth to the back of her mind.
Instead, she pored over the pictures in the
magazine with her mum until the train pulled in
to Victoria Station in London.

As it drew to a halt, Evie craned out of the window and spotted Hannah and her mum waving wildly from the platform. Evie and Mrs Denham picked up their bags, jumped down from the train and rushed over to meet their friends.

'Hello, Julie! Hello, Evie!' called Hannah's mum. 'Phew, it's a bit early, isn't it?'

'Just a bit!' said Evie's mum. 'I think it was still

dark when we had our breakfast this morning, wasn't it, Evie?' Evie grinned and gave Hannah a huge hug.

'I've missed you!' Hannah whispered in her ear before wriggling away to show Evie the piece of paper she was carrying. It was a long list of all the places Hannah wanted to go to that day.

'I've written it all out in order, see?' she said, showing Evie the numbered list. 'The Miss Sparkle Megastore next to Oxford Circus tube station is the first stop. It's the biggest one in the country!' Hannah slipped her arm through Evie's and marched her along the platform. 'Come on, let's go!' she said.

As they walked, a pair of bright red, shiny pumps caught Evie's eye in a shop window. *Beth would love those*, she thought, picturing her friend wearing the cute shoes.

'Hey, Hannah, check out those shoes!' Evie

said. 'Aren't they gorgeous?' Hannah just glanced at them and turned up her nose.

'Not really my style,' she said casually. Evie sighed and bit her lip. *Hannah's a great friend, but she can be really rude sometimes*, she thought.

Chapter Four

Classroom Drama

'**G**ood morning, 5M,' boomed Mr Mitchin on Monday. 'If you could all get out your science books, please ...'

Evie sighed as the class rummaged in their desks for their green exercise books. It only seemed like five minutes since she and Hannah had shared hot chocolates and a flapjack in a café in London. Now she felt like she had fallen back to earth with a bump. She couldn't wait until playtime to catch up with her Crossacre friends, but there was still half an hour to go before then.

Evie soon drifted off into a whirl of memories of adventures with Hannah.

'So, what happens when a solid is heated up?' asked Mr Mitchin. Evie wracked her brains to work out the answer just in case he picked on her. Daydreaming about the new accessories she had bought in Miss Sparkle didn't help much with science!

Luckily, the bell soon rang. Evie leaped up from her chair and ran over to Beth's table to give her a hug and catch up on everything she had missed. But Beth pulled away without a word.

'How was your visit to London?' asked Jess.

'Did you see any celebrities?' added Meera.

'What about the hamburgers?' said Lauren. The

three girls were keen to hear about Evie's
glamorous weekend, but Beth's coldness left Evie
feeling deflated.

'It was great,' said Evie with a weak smile. She
was looking at Beth, who was staring down at
the table. 'What's wrong?' she asked, desperate to
be back on good terms with her friend.

'Nothing,' said Beth, still staring at her desk.

'Come on, there must be something,' Evie continued.

'I said it's nothing!' her friend replied. Evie took a deep breath and mustered up all of her courage. She was determined to get to the bottom of it.

'Is it something to do with Hannah?' she asked. Beth pushed back her chair, red-faced and furious, and ran to the toilets. Evie dashed after her, worried by how upset Beth seemed to be. *There's definitely more to this . . .* she thought.

'Beth?' she said, gently pushing open the toilet door. 'What's up?'

'What's up?' Beth asked angrily. 'I'll tell you what's up. At Malkova's on Saturday, we had to get into pairs to make up a new modern routine for Miss Connie. I really wanted to work with you, so I waited for twenty minutes for you to turn up. Twenty whole minutes!' *Oh, no*, thought Evie, picturing a forlorn Beth waiting at the side of the studio.

'Everyone else had a partner, and Lottie Dean wouldn't stop going on and on about how I had no one to work with,' Beth continued. 'In the end, I had to dance with Miss Connie. She's so much taller than me that we looked really silly dancing together. I was so embarrassed that I ended up falling over my own feet. Everyone laughed and it was all because *you* were in London with *her*!'

Evie felt awful. She thought she had told Beth that she would be missing Malkova's but she must have forgotten in all the excitement. Poor Beth! It was no wonder that she was annoyed.

'Beth, I'm so sorry,' she said, and reached to put an arm around her friend.

'So you should be!' said Beth, her cheeks still flushed with anger. 'Look, can we just drop the

31

whole thing? I don't feel like talking about it any more.'

Beth turned into a blur as Evie's eyes filled with tears. *This wasn't how I imagined today turning out,* she thought.

'And I'd rather that the whole of 5M didn't know about this, so don't bother me about it in the playground either,' Beth said, tilting her chin and leaving Evie alone in the toilets.

Evie put her head in her hands and sobbed. Her day in London with Hannah had been fun, but she had really been looking forward to seeing Beth and telling her how much she missed her. Hannah had been pretty bossy at times, and it had reminded Evie of how much she liked Beth's down-to-earth sense of fun. But it seemed that Evie's forgetfulness had landed her in a sticky situation, with one friend miles away in London, and another who might never speak to her again.

Chapter Five

Disaster Zone

Evie glanced at her watch for what seemed like the hundredth time. *Another hour to go,* she thought, counting down the seconds until she could leave school. It had been a long, hard day and she couldn't wait to curl up under her duvet with her diary. She desperately needed to explain her bust-up with Beth to someone who might be able to help.

Thinking back to the last message from her diary, Evie remembered something about making Beth understand how important Evie felt their friendship was. *It's a good plan*, Evie thought, *but how can I do it when she's not even speaking to me?* She just hoped that her diary could help her find the courage to try another way because, after their awful confrontation earlier, Evie had run out of ideas.

Evie walked alone to the last lesson of the day, food technology. Today, they were going to make bread and Evie had never done that before.

'Come on in, 5M,' called Mrs Fellows, the kindly cookery teacher. 'Please get into small groups and pick a worktop to work at.'

As the class split into groups of four or five, Evie didn't know where to stand. She gulped and stared at the floor while Beth, Jess, Lauren and Meera put their aprons on and headed for a

work area together.

Suddenly, Meera marched over to Evie and grabbed her by the hand. She led her to the work area, checking to see what Beth made of her move. Evie felt her shoulders tense, waiting for Beth's temper to flare up once again. But to her relief, Beth just shrugged and gave a half-nod to show that she didn't mind Evie joining in.

Phew! thought Evie. She knew that Beth wasn't a mean person, just a bit hot-headed at times.

Mrs Fellows gave each of the groups a big blob of dough to knead. Evie pummelled it with her fists, taking out her frustrations of the day on the stretchy mound.

'Excellent work, Evie!' said Mrs Fellows. 'Now try to shape it into a loaf.' Evie pushed and pulled at the lump of dough, but she couldn't make anything that looked even vaguely like a loaf of bread.

'That looks like a giant sausage!' Lauren laughed.

'More like a slug!' added Jess, prodding two dents into the blob to make eyes. The girls fell into heaps of giggles, Beth included, and Evie couldn't help but feel that they were one step closer to fixing up their argument.

'What on earth . . . ?' said a flummoxed Mrs Fellows when she came to collect their dough to rest before baking.

The curious loaf the girls had created was nothing compared to the disaster zone that lay in the other corner of the kitchen. Anthony, Matt and Joseph appeared from a billowing cloud of flour, their hair and uniforms a dusty shade of grey, as they presented Mrs Fellows with their lumpy loaf.

'Eugh!' said Evie with a grimace. 'That looks *horrible!*' She looked cautiously over at Beth to see if she would respond.

'I know!' said Beth. 'You wouldn't catch me eating that even if it was smothered with jam!'

Evie giggled while Meera, Jess and Lauren nudged each other knowingly. Evie wasn't the only one relieved that she and Beth were joking around together again.

As the girls stood side by side at the sink

washing their hands in hot, soapy water, Evie leaned into her friend and said quietly, 'I missed you, Beth. I'm so sorry that we argued.'

Beth looked at Evie for the first time all day.

'Thanks, Evie. I'm really sorry too,' she said. 'I know you didn't mean to forget to tell me about catching an early train. I was just so disappointed that you didn't come to dancing.' Evie grinned as she scrubbed the dough from her fingers. 'What are you up to this weekend?' Beth continued. 'You could come round to mine. We could make fairy cakes together!' Evie's heart sank.

That sounds brilliant, she thought, *but Hannah's coming up to go inline skating!* Evie knew that Beth's feelings towards Hannah were still part of the problem and she just didn't know what to say.

'Um, I'm afraid my mum invited Hannah to stay,' Evie said nervously. Beth's smile disappeared from her freckled face.

'Oh,' she said coolly. 'Never mind. Another time.'

'It's just that we always loved inline skating together, and we got talking about it over lunch at the weekend . . .' Evie tailed off as Beth walked back to the counter where the others were standing. Evie followed, determined not to give up just yet.

'Why don't you come skating too? It would be so much fun!' she asked, forcing brightness into her voice.

'No, thanks,' said Beth.

'Why not, Beth?' asked Meera. 'You love inline skating!' Beth shot Meera a furious look.

'How's your goldfish, Jess?' Beth asked.

Clearly, all conversations about the weekend – and Hannah – were over.

Chapter Six

Bother
at Ballet

Evie peered anxiously through her bedroom
curtains, watching for the Saunders' familiar
blue car in the street. She had felt out of sorts all
week, and having visitors was the last thing on
her mind. She just wanted to hide away in her
room and forget about everything.

School had been very strange. After their
awkward chat in food technology, Beth had been

perfectly nice, but it was clear that she wanted to keep Evie at arm's length. While the other girls had messed around in the playground putting on a talent show, Evie had been left sitting on a bench on her own. Later in the week, Evie had chosen to stay holed up at home, comforted by the wise and friendly words of her magical diary, rather than face a lonely trip to the park.

Stay strong, she remembered the diary had written. *If it's true, your friendship will make it through this test.*

But Evie didn't think that she and Beth would ever get back the sparkling friendship they had had just a few short days ago.

Hopping nervously from foot to foot, Evie searched the street for cars. Last weekend, it had seemed like a brilliant idea to ask Hannah to come down and watch Evie's Saturday dance class before the girls went inline skating around the park together. But now, as Evie's stomach tied itself in knots, it seemed like the visit was only going to make things much worse.

Evie cringed as she pictured the scene: Beth and herself dancing awkwardly together, unable to even look one another in the eye, while Hannah watched from the side, highlighting the distance between them.

When Mr Saunders' car stopped on the driveway, Evie watched Hannah leap out and run to the front door.

Gosh, I wish I was that excited, she thought with a gulp. Hannah was dressed from head to toe in the new clothes that they had chosen together on Oxford Street last weekend.

'Hi, Evie,' she said, a huge grin spreading across her rosy cheeks as Evie opened the front door.

Evie gave the most genuine smile that she could manage and led Hannah up to her bedroom.

'So, what do you think?' said Hannah, striking a pose to show off her new outfit. 'Everyone at school *loved* it. It's all just so *me*, don't you think?'

Hannah chattered endlessly about all of her wonderful new clothes as Evie packed her ballet bag. She was really worried about what Beth would be like when they turned up at Malkova's.

I hope Hannah doesn't notice my funny mood, Evie

thought. *That would only make things worse.*

But Hannah was far too busy telling Evie about how Alice thought her new clothes made her look like a Hollywood star to notice that anything was wrong.

As Evie led Hannah into the foyer at Malkova's, her heart was pounding. Her eyes darted about, looking for Beth.

There she is, thought Evie, spotting her lilac woollen wrap disappearing rapidly towards the other side of the studio. *She must have seen us coming in*, she thought. Determined to be brave, Evie turned to Hannah.

'Come on, there's someone I'd like you to meet,' she said, leading her over to Beth, who was looking rather sheepish. 'Hi, Beth, this is my friend Hannah.' Beth managed a small smile.

'Hi, Hannah, it's nice to meet you,' she replied. But, while she sounded polite, the words didn't quite ring true.

'Hello,' Hannah managed, sounding equally uninterested. Then, Miss Connie came in, clapping her hands to get everyone's attention and interrupting the uncomfortable trio.

Evie ushered Hannah towards a chair at the side of the studio before joining her class for warm-up. She prickled with tension as she did a *port de bras* and some *pliés*.

What on earth am I supposed to do? she thought, longing for her diary.

'Come along, girls,' called Miss Connie. 'Find your partners from last week and continue with the dance that you started then.'

Beth and Evie approached one another, sharing worried expressions. Evie thought back to the fun that they'd had just a couple of weeks ago, making up their lively routine to their current favourite pop song in Evie's bedroom.

It's so different today, she thought as she looked at Beth's serious face.

The girls gripped each other's arms awkwardly, stumbling over their feet as they turned clumsily around their corner of the studio.

'Why don't you two take a break?' suggested Miss Connie, noticing the strain between them. 'Go and have a chat and relax for a few minutes,' she added, gesturing to a couple of spare chairs near to where Hannah was sitting.

Beth took one look and said, 'No, thanks.' She obviously didn't want to spend any time alone with Evie or Hannah. 'We'll just keep going.'

Evie felt churned up inside as they continued their stilted, uncomfortable routine in silence. Beth didn't want to dance with or speak to Evie, let alone get to know Hannah and go inline skating as a threesome.

When Miss Connie announced the end of class, Evie felt relieved. She could barely remember why she normally loved ballet class and usually wished it could go on for longer.

'Come on, Hannah,' Evie said, leading her friend out of Malkova's without even bothering to change. She couldn't get away fast enough.

Chapter Seven

Roller Girls

Evie snapped shut the buckles on her metallic purple inline skates while Hannah found her feet by turning a few circles on the front drive. The girls had spent many afternoons inline skating together before Evie had moved house.

I hope this takes my mind off this morning, thought Evie, who felt sick at the memory of the disastrous ballet lesson.

Hand-in-hand, Evie led Hannah out of the garden and on to the pavement.

The girls could hear a babble of young voices coming from the recreation ground before they even left Oaklands Road. It was a beautiful day and it was teeming with people kicking balls, swinging on the swings and skateboarding on the ramps at the skatepark. They headed for the area next to the skatepark and began to charge about the smooth, flat tarmac.

'Want to race, Evie?' called Hannah, turning pirouettes at super speed.

'Let's sit down for a minute,' said Evie, flopping down on to a bench. 'I want to ask you something about Beth ...'

'We've only just got here!' Hannah said, ignoring the worried tone in her friend's voice. 'Let's race!'

'Hang on,' said Evie, desperate for some advice.

'What do you think I can do to make things up with Beth?'

'Oh, I don't know,' said Hannah, fiddling with the fastenings on her elbow pads. 'Look, an ice-cream van!' Hannah clearly wasn't interested and Evie knew that it was time to snap out of her funny mood.

I'm in the park, in the sun, with my oldest friend, she told herself. *It's time to enjoy myself!*

Hannah was trying to learn how to blade backwards, and watching her pull funny faces as she tried to force her feet in the wrong direction soon had Evie in stitches.

In no time, Hannah was whizzing round and round the tarmac in reverse and Evie just had to give it a try too. She jumped up to join Hannah, leaving her rucksack propped up against the bench.

'Yay, you can do it!' cried Hannah when Evie

had mastered it as well. 'Let's make up some more moves.'

Hannah glided over to the basketball post and, holding on to it with one hand, began to spin around it with one arm waving behind her.

'Brilliant!' said Evie, impressed. She was about to skate over to give it a try herself when she felt a sharp tap on her shoulder.

'Scram!' came a familiar tone. Evie turned to face Lottie Dean, who didn't look happy. 'We're having a picnic here, so you'd better get lost, OK?' Lottie, who was backed up by the ever-snooty Grace and Olivia, folded her arms and waited for Evie to do as she was told.

Evie's stomach tied itself in nervous knots and she stood staring at the trio, lost for words. *Hang on*, she thought, *they haven't even got any picnic stuff with them!* Plucking up every last bit of her courage, Evie stood her ground.

'Why should we go?' she said, her voice faltering a little. 'There's plenty of room for all of us.'

Lottie glared furiously at Evie. She was obviously used to getting her own way. Without taking her eyes off Evie, she grabbed hold of Evie's rucksack and began to swing it around her head.

My diary! thought Evie, remembering how she had carefully packed it into her bag just in case Josh had snooped around her room while she was out.

'Hey!' she cried, leaping up to grab the bag from Lottie's grasp. 'You give that back! It's mine!' Lottie just laughed and swung it harder. The bag windmilled faster and faster and Evie couldn't get hold of it, as hard as she tried.

Evie stared over at Hannah, silently willing her to help. Her friend just stood on the edge of the

56

tarmac, chewing her nails timidly.

A small crowd of children gathered to watch the drama but Evie ignored them. She continued to lurch at her bag, Lottie's cackles growing louder each time she missed it.

Suddenly, a fist burst through the air and snatched the rucksack from Lottie's grasp.

'Give me that!' demanded a boy's voice.

'Oh!' gasped Lottie in surprise, the rucksack whipped from her hand. The nosy kids scattered. Heart pounding, Evie looked up to see who had saved her.

It was her big brother, Charlie! He had stormed over from the skatepark to help out his sister. Evie's eyes filled with tears of relief.

'She took my bag . . . she wouldn't let go . . . everyone watched . . . oh, Charlie!' Evie said, her words falling out in a bundle of sobs and embarrassment. Charlie wrapped her up in a

big-brother hug.

'Come here,' he said kindly. Evie was so
grateful that he had broken his 'no hugs in public'
rule. In fact, he normally didn't even talk to his
sister if anyone from school was around!

'Thanks, Charlie,' she whispered into his T-shirt.
'And thanks for getting Charlie to help me,
Hannah,' Evie said, catching sight of her friend

hovering behind her brother's back. She was looking a bit sheepish, and didn't reply.

'It wasn't Hannah,' Charlie explained. 'It was the girl from your school, Beth, who found me.'

Beth's here? Evie thought, scanning the rec to find her. But she was nowhere to be seen.

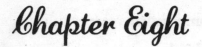

Chapter Eight

A Strange Solution

As Evie waved off Hannah's dad's car on Sunday morning, she felt almost relieved. There was so much that she needed to tell her diary but, because she and Hannah had been sharing a bedroom all weekend, Evie hadn't dared to risk writing in it. She didn't want to even think about what might have happened if Hannah had caught a glimpse of her enchanted book.

She went into her bedroom and slipped her hand into her hiding place for her secret diary: under her pillow. A sparkling feeling ran through her as her fingers grasped the diary's soft velvet cover.

Grabbing her rose-scented gel pen, Evie curled up in the giant, cosy sleepover nest that she and Hannah had built in the middle of her bedroom floor. She couldn't wait to pour her heart out to her diary.

Where do I start? she thought, reminding herself of everything that had happened. She opened her diary and began to write, starting with the awful details about that dance class on Saturday.

Evie filled two pages before she even got to what had happened at the rec. She stopped for a moment to catch her thoughts, nibbling on her pen while a million questions buzzed through her mind. Evie was so grateful to Beth for telling

Charlie that she was in trouble, but why had
Beth left so quickly?

She still doesn't want to be my friend, thought Evie,
missing her more than ever. *But at least she tried to
help me – Hannah just stood in the corner like a mouse!*
Evie knew that Lottie was scary, but still felt
angry with her so-called best friend. She started
writing again.

Then, in the afternoon, Hannah and I went inline skating at the rec. It was awful! Well, it was fun to start with. We practised some brilliant tricks. But then Lottie Dean and the others came and ruined everything. She grabbed my bag, with you inside, and swung it round her head. Everyone else was staring. It was sooo horrible!

I really needed Hannah to help me but she was useless! I understand why she was scared — after all, Lottie is a prize meanie — but I really needed her help and it was horrible to turn round and realise that she wasn't there. I know she felt bad about it too, because she was pretty quiet for the rest of the weekend.

Evie put down her pen and sighed. After the trauma of the last week, she felt washed out. All she wanted to do was hibernate in her bedroom. She put on a CD of soothing ballet music and curled up on the pillows on the floor and tried to forget all of the drama.

A couple of hours later, Evie was lost in her favourite book when her mum popped her head around the bedroom door.

'Hello, love,' she said, putting a glass of apple juice on the table. 'What are you doing up here?'

'Not much,' Evie said. 'I'm just a bit tired.' But Mrs Denham wasn't convinced.

'Why don't you take Josh down to the shop at the end of the road? You could both get a magazine,' she suggested. Evie knew that this was Mum-speak for 'Go outside and get some fresh air!' Mrs Denham always knew when something was wrong, and getting some fresh air was her solution to any problem.

Evie reluctantly wriggled out of her cosy nest, aware that it wasn't worth arguing. If she didn't agree to popping down to the shop, her mum would reel off a whole list of other outdoor suggestions.

Evie found Josh waiting at the bottom of the stairs, clutching a fistful of coins.

'Ready?' Evie asked him.

'S'pose,' replied Josh, who didn't seem too excited by the trip. As the pair trudged out of the house, Evie noticed her mum watching them through the window. She knew that her mum had been so happy when Evie started to make new friends. Now that everything had gone wrong, Evie could tell that her mum was worried about her.

After a quick trip to Nina's News, Josh and Evie walked slowly back up Oaklands Road with a magazine each tucked under their arms.

'Look, Evie, it's that lady from up the road,' said Josh, pointing out Mrs Volkov's silvery head further along the street. They strained their eyes to see what she was doing.

'I think she's reading something,' said Evie. Mrs Volkov beckoned the pair towards her.

'Look, children,' said Mrs Volkov, pointing out a poster that was pinned to a tree trunk. 'It's all about a roller disco in Millchester. What tremendous fun!'

Evie and Josh fought back their giggles as they imagined Mrs Volkov inline skating under flashing disco lights.

'I just like to keep up with what's going on around here, that's all,' she said, dismissing their obvious amusement with a wave of her arm. 'It sounds like a lot of fun. Maybe you should go along, dears.'

Evie couldn't imagine enjoying a roller disco at the moment. She felt like she was stuck underneath a grey cloud. *A roller disco without any friends would be rubbish*, she thought.

Roller
Disco

'Look,' said Mrs Volkov, glancing at Evie. 'The best pair of dancers on the day will win two tickets to see *Waltzing on Ice*,' she read. 'That sounds perfect for you, dear. Now all you have to do is find the right partner.'

Chapter Nine

A Tricky Call

Evie woke early the next morning. She'd shared so many secrets with her diary the day before that she couldn't wait to see its reply. She crossed her fingers and wished for some advice on patching things up with Beth. Her eyes were still half-closed when she pulled the special book from under her pillow. As she opened it, the familiar old-fashioned writing swam into place.

Dear Evie,

Gosh, what a lot has happened! I know it seems like everything has gone wrong, but I am certain that everything will be back to normal in no time. You are a good friend, Evie, and your kindness will win back a troubled friendship. I'm sure that a thoughtful girl like you can come up with a perfect plan to make it happen. Perhaps you'll be inspired by something you have seen . . .

From your diary with love.

The diary was trying to persuade Evie to think long and hard for ways to convince Beth that they should be friends again. Evie's nerves grew as she read the diary's entry over and over again.

Then, as she thought about what had happened over the last few days, she got a great idea. *I know Beth likes inline skating, because Meera mentioned it. And there's a roller disco in Millchester next weekend,* Evie thought. She knew that they would all have great fun if they went together, but there was just one small problem. *If Beth's not talking to me, how on earth can I persuade her to come?* Evie worried.

But she knew she should follow her journal's advice. After all, friendships are about trust, and her enchanted diary had never, ever let her down.

A couple of days later, Evie had a fully formed plan that she began to put into place. She sat at the kitchen table and chatted to her mum.

'Have you seen the poster down the street?' she asked. 'It's for a roller disco at Millchester Leisure Centre.'

'I thought you'd like the sound of that!' said Mrs Denham. 'Why don't you and Hannah go?'

That was easy, Evie thought with a grin. Mrs Denham handed the phone to her daughter, delighted to see her gloominess lifting.

Evie carried the phone up to her room and took a deep breath. She dialled Hannah's number and waited for her friend to answer. Evie knew

that this conversation wouldn't be easy, but she had to be brave if her plan was to work.

'Hi, Hannah, it's Evie,' she said, sitting down on her bed. 'Can you talk?'

'Hi,' Hannah replied, sounding downcast. 'What's up?'

'There's a roller disco in Millchester this weekend and I wondered if you'd like to come,' said Evie.

'Erm, I–I guess so,' said Hannah, uncertainly. She hadn't expected to be invited back to Evie's so soon after Saturday's drama.

'Great!' said Evie, in what she hoped was a bright voice. Deep down, she was really nervous about the next part of the plan. 'There's one more thing. Why don't you bring Alice with you too?' There was a stunned silence from the other end of the phone. 'I know it sounds strange. The thing is, you'll always be my special friend, Hannah.

But now I live in Crossacre, I have other friends too. That's why I'd like to ask Beth to come as my partner to the roller disco.'

'OK,' said Hannah, who still sounded a little unsure.

'Beth is really nice,' Evie continued. 'You saw her at ballet, though you didn't really have a chance to chat.'

'Yes, and she was the girl who went to get Charlie in the park while I stood around and did nothing,' said Hannah, her voice wobbling a bit. 'She seems like a good friend. I wish I had helped, Evie!'

'Don't worry,' Evie said, twiddling her hair around her finger.

'I did have a bit of a funny feeling about her,' said Hannah. 'I know you wanted to talk about your argument at the weekend but I felt a bit jealous. I'm really sorry that I didn't let you talk.'

'Let's forget it,' said Evie. 'I can't wait to see you at the roller disco. We'll be with each other *and* our new friends!' Evie beamed, her excitement shining through her voice.

'Hooray!' said Hannah. 'See you at the weekend!'

Evie put the phone down feeling happier than she had in days. It was great to know that she and Hannah felt the same way about being friends. *We'll always be in each other's lives*, she thought, stretching her legs out on her bed, *but we both know that it's important to have other friends too.*

A few minutes later, Evie remembered one last detail she had to sort out with Hannah. She picked up the phone and pressed the redial button.

'Hannah, it's me again,' she said. 'There's something I forgot to ask you. Can you bring your spare inline skates on Saturday?'

'Of course!' said Hannah. 'I've already spoken

to Alice and she can come too. I can't wait!'

'Great,' said Evie, both relieved and excited that her plan was falling into place. 'I'll see you at the weekend.'

Evie arrived at school a little bit early the next day, hoping to catch Lauren, Jess and Meera before Beth arrived. She ran over to them in the

playground and breathlessly explained her plan.

'I need your help,' she puffed. 'Can you make sure that Beth is at Millchester Leisure Centre at half past five on Saturday?' The girls nodded eagerly, excited to be part of the secret adventure.

Evie hugged herself, realising that the final piece of the puzzle was in place. *Saturday can't come quickly enough*, she thought.

Chapter Ten

Dance Is the Answer

Mr Denham pulled up outside Millchester Leisure Centre on Saturday and Hannah, Alice and Evie clambered out. They were all dressed in bright party clothes and Evie was wearing a full skirt that flew out when she twirled.

They waited nervously by the door for Beth and the others to arrive. The thumping beat of pop music echoed around the leisure centre foyer, and balloons and other decorations hung from every corner. Streams of children glided into the dark gym with luminous bands wrapped around their wrists while the girls put on their blades.

When the beginning of the latest no. 1 chartbuster burst through the speakers, Alice squealed with excitement.

'Why don't you go in? I'll come and find you soon,' said Evie as she leaned in towards Hannah. The pair skated into the gym, hand in hand, while Evie waited outside.

She stepped from side to side nervously in Hannah's spare inline skates. Her own blades, carefully cleaned and threaded with brand new laces, were draped over her shoulder. Evie craned her neck, hopefully looking for Beth and the gang. In the distance, the church clock chimed half-past five. *What if they don't come? I'll be left*

watching Hannah and Alice skate together, Evie worried.

Another two minutes passed and there was still no sign of Beth and the others. Suddenly, two girls shoved past Evie, making her slip on her inline skates. She looked up to see two familiar figures sailing past the learners who were shakily zigzagging towards the doorway. It was Lottie and Grace – but, for once, Lottie didn't stare Evie out or make a smart comment. She just looked away sheepishly. *Wow, that run-in with Charlie might have changed things a bit*, Evie thought.

Just then, Evie heard a loud whistle echo around the leisure centre. *Lauren!* thought Evie. She had never met a girl who could whistle as well as Lauren. Beth, Jess, Lauren and Meera were walking down the road towards the bowling alley! Evie's heart pounded. *They're going the wrong way!* she thought. Then, at the last minute, Lauren and Jess linked arms with Beth and steered her straight towards Evie and the leisure centre.

Beth looked first confused then intrigued by the balloons, decorations and music coming from the foyer. Finally, Beth caught sight of Evie. She looked completely baffled, not even noticing the pair of inline skates that Evie held out for her.

Summoning all of her courage, Evie skated over to meet her friends. Jess, Lauren and Meera grinned and waved at her.

'What's going on?' asked Beth, still confused.

'I know you thought you were going bowling with the girls, but actually, that's not what's going on,' Evie started. 'I wanted to arrange a surprise for you. There's a roller disco tonight and I'd really like you to be my partner.' A small smile appeared on Beth's lips as she took it all in. 'I hope you don't mind us all planning behind your back, but I thought this was the only way that I

could show you just how much I want to be your friend.' Beth beamed as she reached out for the inline skates.

'Brilliant!' she said, lacing up the blades quickly. They fitted her perfectly and Beth was ready to party in no time. The friends put on a luminous wristband each then wheeled into the dark gym.

'Hey, isn't that your friend who visited last weekend?' Beth said to Evie after a couple of laps. Evie caught Hannah's eye and beckoned her and Alice over to join them.

'Hannah, you remember my friend Beth, don't you?' she said.

'Hi, it's so nice to see you again!' said Hannah cheerily. Evie felt proud of Hannah for being so friendly.

'Thanks for inviting me, Evie,' Beth said. 'I missed you this week.'

Delighted, Evie gave Jess the thumbs-up across the room. Things were back on track with both her oldest and her newest friends and she couldn't have been any happier. Until the opening beats of her favourite pop song blasted across the dance floor, that was. Bursting with excitement, Beth and Evie turned to each other and grinned.

They grasped each other's hands and knew that it was time to show everyone what this double act could do. Their dance routine had worked well in Evie's bedroom and they couldn't wait to see how it turned out on wheels. Maybe they would even be in with a chance of winning the prize!

As they threw themselves into their well-rehearsed routine, Evie couldn't stop smiling. Her wonderful, magical diary had helped her to work out a happy ending once again.

Dancing Diva

Impress your friends by learning some of the best ballet moves around!

En pointe

This means to dance on the extreme tip of the toe. There are special shoes to allow you to do this!

Plié

This is the exercise where you bend the knees slowly, with your feet turned out and your heels on the ground. It can also mean bending the knees before starting a jump or landing from a jump.

Rond de jambe

This is a circular movement of your leg, made either on the ground or in the air.

Find more cool ballet moves in the next
From Your Diary With Love book

what's your friendship style?

Bossy boots or quiet chick? Try our quiz to see what you're like!

1. You have concert tickets but your best friend is ill! You...

a Don't go so you can be with her instead

b Go to the concert and tell her how great it was!

c Go and get an autograph for her

2. What does everyone really love about you?

a You're kind and caring

b You always know cool things to do

c You've got the best fashion sense, ever!

3. What do you love most about sleepovers?

a Getting to hang out with your best friends

b Making everyone watch your fave movies

c Showing everyone your cool new pyjamas

4. In the future you really want to...

a Follow your dreams

b Be a superstar

c Have cool clothes

5. If your friend has a problem, you...

a) Help her work it out

b) Tell her to sort it out

c) Tell her all about your problems

6. What sports do you love best?

a) Any sport that makes you part of a team

b) Any sport that you're good at

c) Sports where you can be on your own

Mostly As — Loyal Lady
Just like Evie you're a great mate who is always thinking of her friends. You're quiet, kind and always there for your pals, no matter what!

Mostly Bs — Bossy Babe
Hmm, sometimes you like to be in charge a bit too much, like Lottie! Why not let your friends have a say, it can be fun to try something new!

Mostly Cs — Fickle Friend
You sometimes think of yourself a bit too much, like Hannah. Try thinking about your friends' needs more and it could make you an even better mate!

Ballet Buns

Be a beautiful ballerina with this easy peasy hairstyle!

What you will need:

- 2 elastic hairbands
- Comb
- Hairbrush

What to do:

1. Brush your hair so it's knot-free

2. Now use the comb to make a zig-zag parting

3. Once that's done, separate your hair into two sections, as if you were about to make two bunches

4. Take one side of hair, divide it into three sections and plait them. Then wrap the plait around itself into a snail's-shell type shape. Then secure it with an elastic hairband

5. Now do the same with the other side and then spike out the ends of both buns. Ta da, ballet-tastic!

Marie Taglioni

Be a ballet brain by letting Evie tell you all about one of the world's top dancing talents!

Ballet has been around for a very long time (since the late 1400s) and Marie Taglioni was the greatest ballerina of the Romantic Age. She was born in 1804 and her dad decided she would be a great ballerina. She made her debut at the Paris Opera in 1827 and everyone admired her talent. She was so light on her feet that she looked like she was flying through the air. In 1832 her dad created a ballet called *La Sylphide* for her and she went on to be very famous all over Europe. When she was older she lost most of the money that she had made and she ended up teaching dancing to ladies in London. She retired to Marseilles and died in 1884.

Facts

In Russia people loved her show so much that they cooked and ate one of her shoes after the performance!

La Sylphide was the first ballet where the prima ballerina danced en pointe for the whole performance

She was taught ballet by her father, who was a famous choreographer

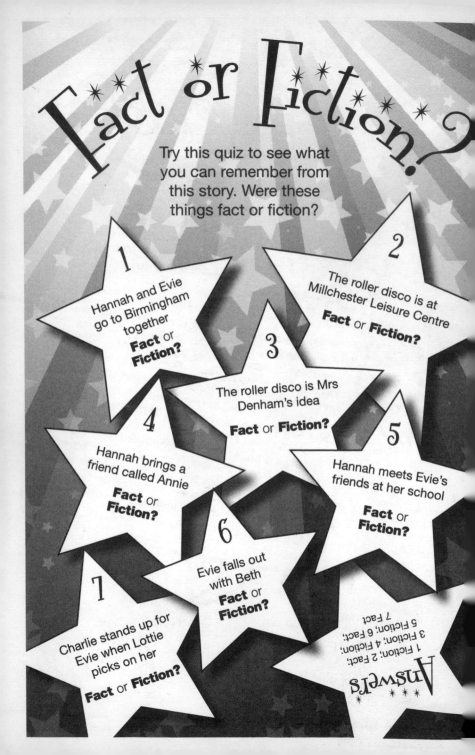

Fact or Fiction?

Try this quiz to see what you can remember from this story. Were these things fact or fiction?

1
Hannah and Evie go to Birmingham together
Fact or **Fiction?**

2
The roller disco is at Millchester Leisure Centre
Fact or **Fiction?**

3
The roller disco is Mrs Denham's idea
Fact or **Fiction?**

4
Hannah brings a friend called Annie
Fact or **Fiction?**

5
Hannah meets Evie's friends at her school
Fact or **Fiction?**

6
Evie falls out with Beth
Fact or **Fiction?**

7
Charlie stands up for Evie when Lottie picks on her
Fact or **Fiction?**

Answers

1 Fiction; 2 Fact;
3 Fiction; 4 Fiction;
5 Fiction; 6 Fact;
7 Fact

Can't wait for the next book in the series? Here's a sneak preview of

From Your Diary with Love

Silence Is Golden

Chapter One

Dancing
on the Edge

Evie stared straight ahead into the mirror and raised her arms into fifth position, above her head, as she prepared to *plié*. A glance to one side revealed that her friend Beth was working hard, too, and the pair bent their knees and dropped into perfect *grands pliés* at the same time.

'Beautiful, children,' said Miss Connie, the young ballet teacher. She was watching Evie and

her friends as they practised their steps in a line at the *barre*. 'Keep those hands soft as you lower your arms down again.'

The atmosphere in the studio at The Malkova Dance Academy was hushed. The students were practising hard to perfect some difficult ballet steps before their exams in a week. Now that the exam date was looming, last-minute nerves had begun to set in.

Evie could hear Beth huff and mutter next to her as she tried to perform the slow movements with grace. Lively Beth preferred fast, fun dancing like jazz and modern, and struggled with some of the more elegant ballet steps.

Meanwhile, Evie was beginning to worry too. She was a born dancer who found mastering the ballet steps came naturally to her. But remembering the complicated French names for them was another matter. Evie just couldn't keep them in her head!

'Mr Jacobs, could you play an *allegro* for us?' Miss Connie called to the pianist in the corner of the studio. 'I'd like you to *grand jeté* across the studio in turn,' she continued as a lively tune echoed around the room. 'Remember: imagine there's an invisible string at the top of your head, lifting you into the air.'

Evie's friend Meera went first, leaping gracefully, as though she were dancing through whipped cream. Next was Matt, the only boy in the class, who managed a reasonable effort despite being a bit gangly. After Matt came Olivia, her brown curls bouncing as she leaped across the room. Then it was Beth's turn but, as she took her very first step, her shoe slipped on the polished floor and she lurched forwards clumsily.

'Oof!' she said, blushing beetroot red as she scurried back to the corner.

'Please begin again,' said Miss Connie gently. Everyone knew that if Beth made a mistake like that in the exam, her chances of passing would be slim.

Evie glared at Lottie Dean, the best dancer (and, in Evie's opinion, the biggest meanie) at Malkova's, who was sniggering unkindly at Beth's mistake. Poor Beth eventually managed to *jeté* across the studio, but her cheeks were still a bit pink by the end of the class.

As the students filed out of the studio and into the changing room, Evie caught up with Beth.

'Don't worry, you'll be fine on the day,' she whispered.

'Fine?' interrupted a loud voice that could only belong to Lottie Dean. 'Bumbling Beth is going to need a lot of help to pass this exam. She looks more like a builder than a ballet dancer!' she said.

Standing in the middle of the changing room, Lottie did a ridiculous impression of Beth's slip-up, her arms and legs flailing everywhere. Her friends Olivia and Grace fell into fits of laughter while Beth bit her lip and stared at the floor.

'What's going on in here?' came a loud voice as a lady bustled into the changing room.

It was Mrs Shanklin, Matt's mum, and her arrival made Lottie pipe down pretty quickly. The girls all knew any mischief that happened in front of Mrs Shanklin would make its way back to their own mothers in no time.

Evie, Lauren, Jess and Meera fussed around Beth, trying to make her feel better, but she was hurt and embarrassed. She stuffed her ballet gear into her bag angrily, eager to pack up and get home. Evie knew that all of her friends were on edge with their exams coming up. They were

working hard on their ballet, but they all had things that they needed to improve on.

We need to build up our confidence before next week, thought Evie. *But how?* Luckily, Evie knew someone who would always help her out with her worries, and she knew that she could share her problems that evening with her secret friend – her magical, enchanted diary.

Enid Blyton's ENCHANTED WORLD

Come and join our exciting adventures!

Can Silky and her fairy friends rescue the magical Talismans lost in the Enchanted World before Talon the Troll finds them?

Read our thrilling stories to find out.

In all good bookshops from September 2008

www.blyton.com/enchantedworld